LOVE'S MIRROR:
A Tragic Romance

LOVE'S MIRROR:
A Tragic Romance

by
Dr. William C.R. Agunwa

Polyverse Publications
Carpinteria, CA United States

Published in the USA by
Polyverse Publications, LLC.
Carpinteria, CA 93013

Paperback ISBN: 978-1-959111-99-3

Contents

1

"Come in, Andrew. Do sit down," Dr. Gordon-Smith, the medical director, said calmly.

Mr. Andrew Wellington was not at all pleased to leave his busy orthopedic out-patient clinic to see the medical director in the Trust Board offices. Sitting next to Dr. Gordon-Smith was Mr. Peter Bruce, the orthopedic clinical director.

Dr. Gordon-Smith continued. "The Head of the Patient and Public Relations Department, Ms. Jane Collins, has received correspondence from solicitors acting on behalf of Ms. Sarah Hopkins and her aunt Mrs. Ruth Drabble. It appears they wish the Trust to investigate a claim against you for improper conduct and for medical negligence. Here is a copy of the letter."

Mr. Peter Bruce, the Orthopaedic Clinical Director, then joined in.

"Unfortunately, the allegations are not as yet terribly specific; however, we would appreciate it if you could give us a factual account detailing your take on the allegations. This will assist our solicitors in defense of the case should it be pursued."

Dr. Gordon-Smith then said, "We may need to instruct an independent expert and would be grateful if you have any recommendations. We understand how busy you are. It would be most helpful, however, if you could give this your early attention."

Mr. Andrew Wellington, an ambitious and driven young surgeon, was known for speaking his mind, even when not politically correct. An Oxford graduate, he was a good rugby player in his time. He was over six feet tall and had dashing good looks. He often let it be known that he was no lover of what he called "bonehead" authority, though, in his late thirties, he had already established an international reputation as a foot and ankle surgeon. He recently returned from a well-subscribed European Foot and Ankle Surgeons (EFAS) conference in Geneva, where he had presented a paper called "Video Photo grammatic Foot Function after Failed Bunion Surgery," which was well received.

Before going to Oxford, Mr. Wellington had been to Downside Public School near Bath on a scholarship. There he was head of Powell House and captain of the school's rugby, hockey, and cricket teams, as well as a member of their renowned Slaughterhouse Seven Jazz Band. His father was a retired army brigadier living near Warminster. While at Downside, he had briefly considered a career in the army after his experience in the school cadet corp.

Mr. Wellington had lost his temper a couple of times on discovering that referrals to him, nationally and internationally, who were not within the catchment area of the Trust had been suppressed by medical records apparently on instructions from high up management to ensure that the Trust met their targets for the department first. He had made his views on the situation known, quite forcibly, to both the clinical director and the medical director.

2

Ms. Sarah Hopkins was a sales manager for an international medical equipment company based in the U.S.A., where she met Mr. Wellington when he went there for an orthopedic conference. They instantly fell for each other.

Ms. Hopkins decided to move in with Mr. Wellington at his luxurious flat in Hampshire when she returned to her native Britain.

On their first outing, Mr. Wellington took Ms. Hopkins to a posh restaurant near Winchester Cathedral. As they drove across a humpback bridge over a local canal near the city central square, Sarah somehow began to muse about the unbreakable midnight curfew her father had put on her evenings out until she turned eighteen. And then he applied the rule with her first proper boyfriend in Durham, Steve Kershaw, as soon as she turned eighteen.

She had met Steve twice in the local pub and spent hours chatting with him. Outside in the yard of the pub, it was fairly dark, dark enough, evidently, for Steve to see nothing against putting his arm carelessly 'round her waist and pulling her half toward him as they stopped by Steve's car.

"You and I are going to get along just fine," he said, all in one low tone.

"I can feel it where it matters!" he said.

With his hand still at her waist, or perhaps her hip, Steve got into the car, which had looked big and dignified at first glance but had turned out to be big and lively. The heavy door creaked and bonked shut.

As they backed 'round, the headlights picked out, apart from a great many other cars, some brick walls topped by iron railings. Then, with a sound like a felled tree beginning to fall over, Steve put the car in gear and almost at once started going very fast. Sarah thought she enjoyed going very fast in cars, even though on the way out she had had to close her eyes once and had reopened them to find they had just missed mounting a pavement. The engine made a lot of noise when Steve was accelerating, and that was what he was usually doing. Sarah accused Steve of being speed mad.

They stopped by a row of terraced houses and got out. Sarah did that on her own before Steve could work up to half-carrying her wherever they might go. But in no time at all, there he was again with his arm diagonally across her back, as if they were in a crowd coming out of a football match and was pressing and nudging her into a gateway.

In the small front garden, she could make out a fair number of artificial ducks, rabbits, and toads, and such exhibits among the imitation crazy paving and the rock plants looked rather grand and interesting in the bright moonlight.

"Don't they look cute!" Steve said, indicating them with one hand while he found his key with the other. This meant he had no hand free with which to touch Sarah, which made a change. He was looking at her frequently, perhaps to make sure of catching her if she decided to make a break for it.

The ride had sobered her up after the gins and tonics and the wine and the cherry brandy, and that was probably just as well, but now that it was coming to a point, she felt a little uneasy. They went up the stairs softly, and Steve opened a door and put on the light. Sarah just had time to notice the room they entered held far more than its fair share of books and magazines before she was grabbed by Steve and passionately kissed. That was all right, in fact, very much better than all right, but it did not go on being all right for very long.

3

The greedy way he murmured, "Ooh, aren't you so lovely? Ooh, aren't you so beautiful? Ooh," into her ear was not quite right as the kiss itself, and the confident suddenness with which he put his hand on her breasts was another matter.

Sarah gripped his wrist. "Don't do that, Steve," she said as soon as she could and leaned back away from him.

He evidently did not hear, going on with his "Ooh, aren't you so beautiful?" line, certain she was enjoying it all as much as he, peering at her with his eyes half shut, then pulling her against him harder than ever, trying to open her finely shaped mouth with his own, forcing his thigh between hers, and finally starting to push his fingers down under the frilly neckline of her dress. Sarah found it difficult to stand there and think things over, about how soon to start trying to slap his face and so on.

Her shoulders went thudding against a wall. When she felt his hand at the zip of her dress, when it appeared she could neither get free nor disengage her mouth to protest, she kneed him gently in the crotch. He winced and let her go at once.

With a heavy, angry expression on his face, made less impressive by the red lipstick that covered most of the lower half of his face, he said, "That was a bit unnecessary, wasn't it?" He was rubbing his lower tummy and nether regions energetically.

"It seemed pretty necessary to me."

"Nobody's done that kind of thing to me before."

"In that case, you've been damn lucky, Steve, if that's the way you usually carry on."

After wiping his mouth on his handkerchief Steve said quietly "I'm sorry, I made a mistake, I thought you were… I'm really sorry, Sarah."

She had been thinking how little she knew him. Now he was familiar again, and she was no longer sure she had tried hard enough to break out of his embrace without causing a fuss. "I didn't really mean to hurt you," she said, "I got scared."

You needn't have been, Sarah, I can assure you, but I can quite see how you were. Very understandable, I must admit. I'm afraid I just got carried away. But I'd soon have realized how you were reacting. I was beginning to, anyway. I wouldn't have gone on much longer in that strain even if you hadn't… taken action! Bad thing to get carried away of course, but people do, you know." He seemed over it now; he was giving reasons, having a discussion with her.

She looked at him softly and sadly. "Yes, I know."

"You were quite justified. I deserve it, Sarah. Don't be angry. Don't go. I promise I'll behave myself."

She thought she should go. But it would look so silly, so high and mighty. And deep down, she knew she could not bear to go, not now, not when she had only just got to know him. And after all, what was she committing herself to merely by staying? She could walk out any time she felt like it.

"All right," Sarah said to Steve, "but mind you do, now."

He grinned broadly, stepped actively forward, and took her yielding soft hands. To recoil now would be ridiculous and silly. "That's my girl." He sighed comically, blowing out his cheeks, winking, and dilating his eyes.

"I really thought I'd had it for good then, honestly. What an idiot I was! Well, now, what about… just to show there's no ill feeling…"

Steve kissed Sarah again, but it was quite different: calm and gentle and without him having to push his tongue into the back of her throat to show how keen he was. It was really much nicer like this. All that tongue work was very overrated and, when you come to think about it, rather rude as well. Probably it was a thing people went in for because it was the fashion, not so much because anybody was meant to like it.

Anyway, Steve's mouth was curved just the right amount and soft without being squashy, with a good sort of washed smell. The kiss started going on and on, rather, but Steve was the one who finally stepped back, saying, "That was more like it, eh?"

"Possibly," she said, smiling.

"You know, you really are the most… but we've been into all that, haven't we? Now I know, what you'd like now. Bet you. A nice cup of coffee."

"Ooh, lovely, yes, please."

"There you are. Always trust a Kershaw hunch and intuition."

"Could I go to the bathroom?"

"Well, yes, if you insist. I'm afraid you won't think it's a very nice bathroom."

4

It wasn't. Sarah repaired her mouth, using a mirror that could do with a bit of cleaning. She finished her coffee. Steve looked down at her with renewed admiration. It was just about time for kissing to come 'round again, and very soon, after he had bent slowly downwards and sideways from his chair, it did. It was gentle and great. Sarah began to feel warm and dreamy.

Then Steve said, "I'm sorry. This is hellishly uncomfortable. I wonder… I can't really reach you there. Do you think you could come and sit on my lap?"

I don't know," Sarah said. "I'm not much of a one for bottoming on men's laps."

"I'm not men, you silly darling. Come on. It'll be all right. Honestly. Just you see."

If Sarah had not had at the back of her mind the feeling that a man who had bought her drinks on that night's scale was entitled to some return and a bit further back still the fear of being thought high and mighty, she would not have hoisted and edged her way with the awkwardness of a tourist mounting a camel in Gaza, on to Steve's lap. But she did.

Ages seemed to go by. As well as the actual kissing, there was the stroking, neck, and ears to begin with, which were very rousing. Sarah felt dreamier and more abstracted than ever. Then he took his mouth away, but not far. She was becoming a bit more assertive and rubbed her cheek against his.

"You're a nice kisser," she said.

He evidently did not hear this. At any rate, he made no reply, just said, "Darling," with a breathy sigh, and started kissing her again.

Soon his hand slid 'round under her armpit and climbed onto her left breast. This time she let it stay there. She always welcomed a decent build-up first. She let him play with her nipple.

Before long Steve slipped his left hand under her dress in the non-important places: back, shoulder, upper arms. Soon his hand, moving sort of sleepily, began trying it on at the front. Very slowly he moved from her tummy button to between her thighs but shied away from her thong knickers.

After this they went the rounds again from the scratch, this time with Steve trying less routine things like ear-nibbling and neck-nuzzling and small-of-the-back massaging. Suddenly Sarah went all soft and yielding, lifting up the hem of her dress considerably and parting her thighs widely, then crossing and uncrossing her legs provocatively.

But then he tentatively tried to stroke her luxuriant ebony bush under her skimpy thong, she shifted her position, took his wrist, and said in a coughly bass and magisterial voice, "Enough! When I say no, I mean no."

Steve sat up with his arm still 'round her but differently. "Are we going to go on like this all night?" he asked in a conversational voice.

"I don't know about all night. I'll have to be getting back soon."

"Hell, why wouldn't you let me do what I was trying to do just then? It wasn't anything very serious, was it? It wasn't as if I was asking you to strip or do table dancing, was it?"

"Of course not, but you know how one thing leads to another."

"But there wasn't going to be another, I told you that."

"So you say. There always is another. And with this kind of thing, it gets harder and harder as you go on to tell where one leaves off and the next begins. And there is no game to beat this for changing minds."

"A fine piece of feminine doublethink and arcane logic, that."

"Call it what you like."

"All right, I'll take you home. We've both had enough for one night."

As they left and got into the car, no pulling and pushing to and fro this time, Sarah felt mildly depressed.

They eventually drew up outside Sarah's place. She darted out of the car and gave him a wave as he drove deafeningly away.

5

Andrew and Sarah's meal at the Winchester restaurant went very well. Drinks apart, they had rhubarb soup, salad with smoked chicken, and mango and white asparagus, followed by buttermilk sorbet and *millefeuille* of nougatine and fresh berries.

They went back to Andrew's flat, rather pleased with themselves, and made love with tenderness and abandon. For months they seemed to live in a world of their own until Sarah had to fly back to New York for the launch of a new surgical laser "knife" product.

Andrew missed Sarah badly. He had a reputation, however, for a winning way with good-looking women, especially young daring ones like Helen, a newly appointed radiographer at one of the peripheral hospitals where he had a weekly Thursday afternoon clinic session. After one trying overbooked and single-handed clinic at Helen's hospital, with many "missing" X-rays and unusual delays in patients having their follow-up X-rays, Andrew bumped into Helen in the main hospital corridor on his way home at the end of the clinic session. They apologised to each other profusely, exchanged knowing glances and agreeable smiles. They had exchanged glances a few times before on that same corridor.

Andrew invited Helen for a drink that evening at a local pub, and she eagerly accepted. They ended up in Andrew's flat, and Helen spent the night there.

Sarah decided to return to the U.K. from New York earlier than expected and with her duplicate key to the flat, she gently opened the door and walked in to find Andrew and Helen in bed, their underclothes all over the floor, their naked torsos exposed with Helen's left arm across Andrew's waist and her face resting beatifically on Andrew's hirsute chest.

At first Sarah could not believe her eyes. She coughed politely. Andrew and Helen quickly woke up, Helen folding her arms reflexively across her breasts. Andrew kept his eyes shut while Sarah looked at him with steely eyes and cold disdain, totally ignoring Helen. With consummate dignity, she packed her things and left, not uttering a word.

6

The next day, Sarah wrote to Andrew's NHS Hospital Trust with two main complaints against him: firstly, that Andrew had given the Trust a false account of the cost of the high-resolution, lightweight newest ankle arthroscope purchased from her company for the orthopaedic department. And also that Andrew was contracted, for a considerable fee, to be on their payroll for his feedback on foot and ankle implants and instruments. Secondly that her aunt, Mrs. Ruth Drabble, just turned sixty, was shabbily treated and mismanaged under Andrew's care following her right wrist fragility fracture. She now had a very deformed and painful wrist. Despite requests from her worried husband, Andrew had not bothered to look into her case.

Additionally, she had sustained, a few days back, a fragility fracture of the neck of her left femur, which turned out to have a myeloma lesion, common in osteoporosis. They were all the more aggrieved because of the Trust had a nurse practitioner with interest in this type of fracture. She acted as a link with local general practitioners in ensuring that patients with fragility fractures were properly investigated and treatment initiated as indicated. No such referral was made in respect of Mrs. Ruth Drabble.

The following week, Mr. Andrew Wellington was summoned to the Trust Board offices once more and told he was being suspended with full pay until further notice, on the orders of the Hospital Chief Executive, Mrs. Margaret Cribbin. He was to remove his belongings from his office under escort by the hospital security staff and leave the hospital premises forthwith.

The Trust then went into overdrive to discredit Mr. Wellington professionally. A replacement locum was appointed. The medical director asked the orthopedic clinical director to review all of Mr. Wellington's cases for the past couple of years. They wrote to Mr. Wellington's patients, inviting their comments on what they felt about Mr. Wellington. A dossier was to be prepared, leading to a formal submission to the General Medical Council, accusing Mr. Wellington of serious professional misconduct.

7

The letter from the chief executive to Mr. Wellington said:
In the normal course of events, Dr. Gordon-Smith, the medical director, will now proceed to collate information on your clinical practice from clinical staff within this Trust. This together with other reports will go forward to the General Medical council... Additionally, following representation from Dr. Gordon-Smith, an alert letter has been issued by the NHS executive of this region. This will ultimately reach all trusts in the United Kingdom. We have a concern about your practice. If any other organisation approaches me with a view to appointing you to a position within their healthcare organisation, then I am obliged to inform them of the events that have happened within this Trust.

Mr. Wellington contacted his Medical Defence Union straight away. Its medical adviser wrote to Mr. Wellington's Trust, asking for a meeting to discuss matters. The Trust was initially disinterested. Eventually a rapid response team from the Royal College of Surgeons in London was invited. Later a panel of four assessors from the General Medical Council also came to investigate. The lead assessor was a general practitioner, and then there were a lay assessor, an ex-police superintendent, a medical assessor, and an additional orthopaedic surgeon assessor.

A few months later, Mr. Wellington got a letter from the General Medical Council's assistant registrar in a "Confidential Special Delivery" envelope, stating that in the light of the information received, Mr. Wellington's case coordinator had now referred his case to the GMC's Committee on Professional Performance.

The letter went on:

It is the function of the committee on the Professional Performance to consider and decide whether the standard of the professional performance of the doctor concerned has been seriously deficient. Where the committee finds that a doctor's professional performance has been seriously deficient, the committee will either impose conditions on the doctor's registration for a period of up to three years or suspend the doctor's registration for a period of up to twelve months. In either event, the committee will then resume its consideration of the case before the end of the period of conditional registration or suspension, and will decide whether to impose any further sanction on the doctor's registration.

The letter continued:

Where, on the other hand, the Committee on Professional Performance concludes that the standard of a doctor's professional performance has not been seriously deficient; the GMC will take no further action in that case. The committee also has the power to direct that a further assessment of your performance be carried out and to suspend or impose conditions on your registration if you then fail to comply with the reasonable requirements of the Assessment Panel.

Hearings of the Committee on the Professional Performance are conducted in private, unless the doctor concerned requests a public hearing. You will be notified at least twenty-eight days beforehand of the date on which the Committee on Professional Performance will consider your case. You will be invited to attend the hearing, at which you may also be represented or accompanied by an officer of any professional organization of which you are a member or by a member of your family. In addition, if you so wish, you may be accompanied by a medical adviser.

8

Prior to the GMC panel visiting Mr. Wellington's Trust, the panel had received a set of documents from the GMC consisting of:

-The portfolio completed by Mr. Wellington
-Correspondence between the GMC and Mr. Wellington
-A letter from Mr. Wellington's Medical Defence Union to the GMC
-A curriculum vitae of Mr. Wellington
-A report to the GMC from Mr. Wellington's Trust
-A report from the rapid response team of the Royal College of Surgeons
-A copy of the alert letter produced by the NHS executive concerning Mr. Wellington
-A set of documents relating to Mr. Wellington's suspension from his Trust hospitals
-Statements from some of Mr. Wellington's colleagues and other medical and nursing staff.

Preparatory to Mr. Wellington's assessment, the GMC assessors had initial discussions by telephone followed by a meeting to review the documentations and agree on specific areas to be explored during the assessment. During the course of the assessment, the panel met frequently to discuss progress and address any issues arising.

Thirty medical records of patients who had been under the care of Mr. Wellington were reviewed. The records were selected so as to contain a range of typical conditions dealt with by Mr. Wellington. The records were reviewed by the medical assessors with guidance from the lead assessor. It was not possible to observe clinical practice as a result of Mr. Wellington's suspension from his consultant post.

In writing their final report, the assessors took account of Mr. Wellington's written response to their third-party interview transcripts.

The report was based on the headings of good medical practice issued by the General Medical Council. Except for matters of fact, the panel reached a conclusion only when there were at least three sources ("triangulation") and after giving due consideration to the weight of each contribution.

Each judgment was recorded using the following scale:

A =Acceptable
C = Cause for Concern
U= Unacceptable

9

It took quite a few months after the assessors had reported before Mr. Wellington's case was listed for hearing at the GMC offices, Committee Suite, 178 Great Portland Street, London. In the interim, Mr. Wellington had been invited on a well-paid lecture tour of the U.S.A, where he was very highly regarded.

In New York, he stayed at the Royal Manhattan Hotel, and from there he traveled to the Hospital for Special Surgery, where he gave two talks called "Total Ankle Replacement-An Overview" and "The Charcot Foot-Cytokine Bone Resorption the Primary Event?"

Andrew Wellington went down to the coffee shop on the ground floor of the Royal Manhattan Hotel one morning. He got a jolt and a shock when a young lady walked in, and she looked uncannily like Sarah Hopkins. Andrew had tried hard to blur the image of Sarah, which suddenly ignited itself in his mind at the sight of this woman.

That long, shining stream of dead-straight auburn hair; that smooth, shiny skin; that tough, tender mouth; those small but high and noticeable breasts; those delicate, oblong wrists; and above all, worse than anything else for some unfathomable reason, those quick, nervous movements, plus that steady, steely gaze….

Andrew, after his break-up with Sarah Hopkins, forced himself to make a vague resolution to abstain from all woman-dealings. He thoughtfully marveled at the size, number, variety, and extraordinariness of the hoops through which females made their male counterpart jump, wittingly or otherwise.

But his resolution seemed to crumble when the young lady sat near his table in the coffee shop. Andrew ran his eye over the well-finished and engaging figure of a woman before him.

"Cigarette to smoke?" Andrew unexpectedly found himself offering.

"No, thanks," She said softly, flashing a smile at Andrew.

What bedroom-eyes! Andrew said to himself. "Excuse me," Andrew said weakly as he moved to a counter to acquire a box of chocolates. "Would you like a chocolate?"

"Thank you very much. What a pretty box," she said.

"You know, you seem to have a very sweet nature," Andrew ventured. "And you're very beautiful. You have a charming, sensual face and good hands, and your figure is adorable."

"That's nice of you," she responded with uncharacteristic shyness. "Can I have another of the chocolates? They're ever so good."

She was a little ashamed of being embarrassed by his compliments. She stole a glance at him with a half-smile. Then her smile broadened.

They looked at each other, and Andrew excitedly asserted, "Three guesses and I'll get your name right."

"Don't bother. You'll never get it."

"It's Alison, isn't it?"

"How on earth did you know?"

Alison felt a thrill that was almost a shiver. Her body tensed. She noticed that Andrew's eyes were wider than usual, as though he was surprised about something. She beamed at him.

Andrew had noticed the initials "AH" embossed on her Italian leather handbag and declaimed the first name starting with the letter "A" that came to his head: the name of his first girlfriend at Oxford.

At the far end of the coffee shop, Alison stole a glance at a couple kissing each other. Their bodies were tightly pressed together, and Alison could hear the faint rustling as he stroked her hip. Then she heard the sound of a load wheedling noise made by the separating mouths of the couple, the man then lowering his face to nuzzle her neck.

"Alison, you seem miles away," Andrew commented. "Are you all right?"

"I'm all right," she replied unconvincingly. She had felt an intense frisson watching the couple. She impulsively took Andrew's right arm and said, "Let's go for a loop drive of the Big Apple. My Merc sports car is just 'round the corner. No three guesses that you are a very English visitor to this "City That Never Sleeps.""

The drive took them to Central Park, Lincoln Centre, the Theatre District, Rockefeller Plaza, Radio City, St. Patrick's Cathedral, Fifth Avenue, the American Museum of Natural History, the Cathedral of St. John the Divine (still awaiting completion,) Apollo Theatre, Harlem neighborhoods, The Metropolitan Museum of Art, Guggenheim, the Empire State Building, Greenwich Village, Soho, Little Italy, Chinatown, the Financial District, Battery Park, Times Square, and then the United Nations.

Andrew especially felt exhilarated, if not exhausted, by the drive. He was very impressed with Alison's driving skills. They finished up at Alison's apartment for coffee.

In the corridor leading up to Alison's apartment, Andrew mused at a painting of an oversized girl with oversized hips wearing a diaphanous shift dress, and with an oversized face that had an oversized chin on it in a provocative sexual pose.

"How stunning!" Andrew commented, tongue in cheek.

"No comments, Andrew," Alison said demurely.

"Ssshh," Alison stage whispered as they approached her apartment.

Almost scared now, her mind rehearsed formulas of conscience and discretion while Andrew's right hand softly petted her behind. She felt her cheeks going hot. She leafed rapidly through her memory of romantic involvements, and there was nothing quite like what she was beginning to feel for Andrew.

They finally arrived at her apartment. She said in a muffled voice, "Do come in, Andrew. Excuse the mess on the table."

As they sat next to each other on the sofa-bed in nervous silence, Alison got very absorbed daydreaming about Andrew making a masterful move… grabbing her abruptly and efficiently, firmly enough in a sort of diagonal lock, hanging on to one shoulder and bringing her 'round by pulling politely at a bit of her other hip, then kissing her fully on the mouth….

But one thing had the habit of leading to another, and often before you knew where you were, too, and although she could eagerly go with this thing all right, she wondered if she would uninhibitedly go for the other, and the one after that….

She came to suddenly as Andrew nudged her gently, saying, "Anyone there?"

Alison made a point of never thinking about marriage, feeling it might be unlucky to do so. But deep down, when she first met Andrew, she had said to herself, "That's the one!"

She felt awkward and unusually subdued: *I don't know that he's the marrying kind,* she thought faint-heartedly.

10

Alison slipped one of her hands into Andrew's and looked him straight in the eye, trembling a little. He responded by interlocking fingers with her and gently pressing his thumb into the palm of her soft, yielding hand. She got up, still holding hands with Andrew, drew the curtains, and made the move to the bed. They lay down on top of her new bedspread and began to kiss.

When their kissing reached one of its climaxes, she felt, as she often did, like making some little satisfied, appreciative noises and was only held back by the thought, based on experience, that such noises were liable to act like a red flag, or rather a green light, to a bull.

Andrew slipped his hand down the front of her dress. Her seemingly small breasts under her dress had swelled surprisingly to be handfuls. Lying in his arms, his mouth and hands so gentle now and his clean smell so wonderful, Alison realised the things you read about being in love were not exaggerated or silly as she had once suspected, but quite literally true. It could change your whole life. It gave you all sorts of new feelings you would have no idea existed otherwise about work and other people and the weather and the time of day and the look of the town and the thought of places all over the world you had never been to (they mean more: you could imagine all the foreign-looking buildings and the men and women, boys and girls, crowding along the streets) and records and food and drink-stuff not really connected with love at all. She had a sort of permanent glass or two of champagne inside her.

The kisses started mounting up again. They filled her with warmth and strength and confidence. Soon this started to feel like not keeping still, getting friskier and wanting to change over to a different style of breathing, doing something out of character.

Just then, Andrew's hand made its next move, the one that could take her over the abstract line she had drawn. She was not then wearing any knickers. She removed his hand from between her thighs, a job that took rather longer than usual, as she regretted more and more deeply having to draw the line.

She knew he could tell how passionately she wanted him to make real love to her, and his never using this to try and persuade her made him even more marvelous. If this was courting, what would marriage to Andrew be like? This was not a thought to dwell on.

In a moment, she whispered, "Darling, what about that cup of coffee we came up her for?"

Andrew sighed, but it was a mild, non-peevish one. "Okay, Delilah!"

She saw his face come back to normal from its heavy, drowsing look, sensing that he had traveled further away from the here and now than maybe she had and so took longer to return. Alison put her arms around his neck and kissed him.

11

Alison came over to the U.S.A from England with her twin sister when their father in the diplomatic service was posted to Washington. She attended Harvard Business School and was now a high-flying Wall Street fund manager. At her workplace, she was highly respected, if awe-inspiring, for her single-mindedness and uncompromising pursuit of details. And she did get impressive results.

But since meeting Andrew, her emotions had been all over the place. She would come back from work and curl herself up tightly in bed, trying to think about Andrew. Being kissed by him was getting more and more extraordinary all the time. She would relax during her think about him, and then she would feel completely alone.

Today everything was quiet and cheerless. There was not even enough breeze to stir the curtains. Unhappiness used up energy faster than anything. In the semi-darkness, the furniture of her apartment, which had such a pleasant, welcoming look when she came on it by day, seemed squat and heavy and just dumped down where it was, as if she was in bed in the corner of a warehouse.

She was also struggling to forget a drunken pass made at her at an office do by a filthy-rich balding foreign client.

"Well, well, well," he said heartily, "Look what the wind's blown in. Alison in person, eh?"

Alison smiled weakly.

"What about kissing me goodnight?" he persisted.

"Oh, I don't know if that would be a very good idea, would it? I don't think you're in the state to get the best out of it."

"You can say what you like. I don't care what you say like… what you… say like. I've kept my hands off you for too long, and I'm not going to miss out now. Not… going to miss…"

He lurched diagonally forward and over her, his hands thudding down on the arms of her chair. His face searched for hers, weaving to and fro like a hungry fish. Alison folded her arms over her bosom and dug her chin into her shoulder. She could tell now he had indeed been mixing his drinks. All the times she laughed in the jolliest way she could, searching her memory for all the funny things that had ever happened to her. She tried to keep up the laughing when the client found the edge of her mouth and began squirming his own mouth along it, caterpillar-fashion, toward the middle, but laughing into someone else's mouth is hard work, she found, especially when their arms give way and they squash down on your chest.

The broad tip of his nose was against hers, too, pushing it far enough 'round the corner to cut her air-intake by half. She tried to focus her vision and lost no time in unhitching his pair of glasses from his ears.

He made a desperate lunge, lost his balance, and spun under a table. Too breathless for any more laughing, Alison went and gave him a hand, and when he was just about on his feet, she disappeared.

12

The next day, Alison had a call from Andrew.

"How about a holiday break in the Caribbean?"

"Oh, God," she said. "I'd hate it like poison, you bet I would. Oh, Andrew, could we really?"

"It's only up to you to fix it with your office."

"Separate rooms, Andrew," she said teasingly. "It'll be wonderful to get away from here ASAP!"

The next day, Andrew and Alison flew off to the "Platinum Coast" of West Barbados, renowned for its white beaches and exuding an atmosphere of sophistication and elegance with majestic hotels lining the coast running from Bridgetown to just beyond Spreightstown in the North. They booked into a four-star hotel on the outskirts of Holetown, which was the first settlement in Barbados. The hotel had an enviable location, with well-appointed rooms overlooking the ocean and promised a quiet respite from the world where they just escaped.

The hotels pools were set in a lush tropical garden and had pool bars. Their apartment had a spacious balcony, a whirlpool bath, satellite television, and a king-size bed. The hotel boasted at least eight hours of beautiful sunshine every day, cuisine to suit every taste and a perfect dining experience, sunset cruises, scuba diving and snorkeling, windsurfing, flood-lit tennis courts, a first-class eighteen-hole golf course, an air-conditioned gymnasium, water sports, a spa, relaxing massage parlours, and regular live music and entertainment. Or you could simply take things easy and chill out on the wonderful beach. There was a veritable melting pot of nationalities at the hotel.

Andrew and Alison spent their first day in Barbados scuba diving and snorkeling followed by a sunset cruise. That gave them a healthy appetite for their room service late supper. And so to bed.

"Not a bad day for starters, Andrew," Alison remarked.

"Splendid, I'd say," he replied.

"I feel absolutely but happily knackered."

"So am I, Alison."

"Do you *really?* You know…."

"You've got such a filthy mind!"

"Me? Never! I'm a well-brought-up convent girl."

"Ha, ha, ha! They are often the worst!"

"I'll show you, idiot!"

To Andrew's amazement, Alison very deftly flipped away the bed coverlet, pinned him on the bed spread-eagled, pulled off his pajama's bottoms and demanded that he beg for mercy.

"Bond girl, eh?"

"Beg for mercy, or else!"

Before she could continue, Andrew half extricated himself from his compromised position, but Alison wasn't going to let go so readily. They finished up in a most intimate tangle with Alison's shortish and clingy black silk sleepwear on the floor.

They kissed and kissed and kissed. Their lips and hands explored and explored. They tumbled into the softly carpeted floor naked, still entwined and almost breathless, *body surfing.* They stopped short of going all the way.

They fell asleep on the floor. Alison awoke slowly, her eyes opening like a winter morning, her pink lips parted, the whole of her warm, soft, serene, and friendly, Andrew looked at her awestruck and hopelessly in love with her. He kissed her gently and thought her mouth as sweet as fresh herbs.

"I'll go to the bathroom first," Alison murmured, half awake.

"No, you won't" Andrew teased.

"Don't you tell me, fellow."

"Don't be long, then."

"I'll be back when I'm quite ready, thank you very much." She kept her word.

"I'm getting up now," she said after a minimal pause.

"Oh, don't do that yet. It's so very nice as things are."

"I'm going to have a bath."

"I'll come and have a shave and talk to you."

"You will not. There are times when I like to be alone."

While Andrew shaved later, he thought about the precious night with a smile. The addition of a look of sweetness to a look of intellect, inventiveness, and beauty was overwhelming. He suddenly found himself singing Nat King Cole love songs to himself…. *"You Stepped Out of a Dream…"* *"Unforgettable…."* *"I'm in the Mood for Love…"*

13

Andrew and Alison's week in Barbados went very quickly. They tried their hand at most of the facilities available at the hotel, including windsurfing, water sports, flood-lit tennis, a few rounds of golf, gym workouts, and the spa, plus Alison spending quite some time at the massage parlors. They swam every morning in the splendid pools followed by long, amorous chats over drinks at the pool bars.

The day before they flew back to New York, Andrew proposed to Alison on bended knees on the balcony of their hotel suite after their morning swim. He needed some stiff drinks beforehand.

"Alison, will you marry me, will you?"

"Of course I will. I thought you'd never ask. Get up, stupid, or you'll fall over the balcony in your drunken crapulent state."

They married the next morning in Barbados by special license in a civil ceremony. The wedding near the tropical gardens of the hotel was free excluding the administration charge by the hotel. And the hotel toasted them with complimentary champagne, flowers, and a celebration dinner at the Garden Restaurant.

When they got back to New York as blissful man and wife, it was a stunned Andrew who slowly realized from Alison's family photo albums they were leafing through that

Alison Hopkins, his new bride, was in fact the twin sister of his former lover, Sarah Hopkins.

For now, the troubling shock must be kept under wraps, Andrew said to himself. He was too much in love with Alison to have anything, even this, disturb their trance.

The next day, they went shopping on Fifth Avenue and, among other things, talked about how many children they were going to have. They decided on two, a boy and a girl, possibly. If a third happened, no problem. Andrew moved in with Alison at her modest but well-appointed apartment in midtown Manhattan, north of Grand Central Station and close to the theatres on Broadway.

14

Waiting for Andrew on his return from Barbados was a letter from the General Medical Council advising him on the date for his appearance before the GMC's Committee on Professional Performance. Andrew discussed the situation with Alison without mentioning the part her twin sister, Sarah, had played in his being reported to the General Medical Council.

"You must have the best legal representation, a leading counsel, a top queen's counsel, whatever the cost. I know a good lawyer can make all the difference," Alison insisted.

Even though Andrew's Medical Defence Union used a firm of renowned solicitors in London for GMC quasi-judicial hearing, Andrew and Alison went ahead and secured the services of a highly sought-after leading counsel, Mr. Edward Powell-Jackson QC of Exchange Chambers, and they happily made a down payment of £15,000.

Maybe it was twin telepathy, but it wasn't long before Sarah got wind of the fact that the man her twin sister married in Barbados was in fact her former lover. She was even more determined than ever to get even with him, or better still, ruin his career irreparably.

There always had been an intense sibling rivalry between Sarah and Alison, and even at birth, Alison had managed to grip Sarah as she emerged first. They were both go-getters and hated to be bested by anyone, especially since coming over to the U.S.A from England with their diplomat father.

Damn it! Sarah exclaimed to herself. *If he thinks he can use me then marry my sister like that, he has another thing coming.*

Sarah had supplied to Andrew's hospital Trust the details of the alleged false accounting in Andrew's medical equipment purchase from her, which was one of the main reasons for his suspension, though his aggressive stand against management for instructing medical records to withhold national and international referrals to him that might get in the way of meeting departmental targets was probably a greater factor.

In its letter, the GMC informed Andrew that the hearing of his case would begin at 9:30 A.M. on a Wednesday in the Committee Suite, 178 Great Portland Street, London. He was to report to fourth-floor reception at 9:00 A.M. to be escorted to the Committee Suite.

The Committee met in private unless stated that you would prefer a public hearing. No information about individual cases was published, unless and until a doctor's performance was found to have been seriously deficient.

The following people attended the hearing:

The members of the Committee (about seven people, including at least one lay person, all of whom are GMC members.)

At least one specialist medical adviser. Specialist medical advisers were not GMC members. They were doctors whose names were put forward by professional bodies. Their task was to advise the Committee as necessary in relation to the type of medical practice in which you specialise or had recently been working.

A legal assessor, a senior barrister who advises the Committee on any legal issues that may arise.

The Committee secretary, who is a senior member of the GMC staff.

It is for you to decide what you or your representative
wish to say to the Committee when the chairman invites you
to address the Committee. You may find it helpful, however,
to know that the Committee will have read all the papers in
the case that the GMC has sent to you for the hearing. It will
be familiar with your case and will not require you to remind
it of the history.

It is open to you to call any witnesses to whom you
would like to give evidence on your behalf. If you choose to
call anyone, it will be your responsibility to arrange for them
to attend.

In addition, if you wish to question any of the people
who are the authors of documents included in the case papers,
you can ask the GMC to arrange for them to attend the hearing as witnesses. It is best first to consult your representative
on this point.

15

The GMC had undertaken third-party interviews, including Mrs. Sarah Hopkins and Andrew's NHS Trust, during Andrew's suspension. They had assessment judgments as either:

    A =Acceptable

    C = Cause for Concern

    U= Unacceptable

in regard to Andrew's performance, especially in these areas of interview of third parties:

-Respect for patients, trust, and confidentiality
-Educational activities
-Constructive participation in audit, assessment, appraisal
-Providing or arranging treatment
-Working within limits of competence
-Working within laws and regulations
-Arranging cover, delegation, and referral
-Relationships with colleagues/ GP's/ teamwork
-Treatment in emergencies
-Teaching and training
-Providing or arranging investigations
-Assessment of patient's condition
-Communication with patients.

The chairman of the hearings was Professor Ian Farting-Bottom, a general surgeon. Andrew was represented by Mr. Edward Powell-Jackson QC, instructed by Mr. Appleby, a solicitor from the firm of solicitors in London engaged by his Medical Defence Union. The lay members of the GMC on the panel included a general practitioner, who apparently had a thing about hospital consultants, a female social worker, and a known campaigner for patients' rights.

After Andrew had taken his oath on the Bible, the chairman introduced the members of the Committee sitting around the long and broad oblong and well-polished table. A bottle of water and a drinking glass was provided for each one sitting around the table.

The GMC's solicitor got the proceedings underway by presenting the case against Mr. Andrew Wellington with professional detachment. He was standing, almost directly opposite Andrew, who was flanked by his leading counsel, Mr. Edward Powell-Jackson, and his solicitor, Mr. Appleby. The medical adviser, Dr. Adrian Bolt, from his Medical Defence Union sat next to Appleby. The chairman sat at one end of the oblong table to Andrew's left, and the other end of the table was unoccupied.

The rest of the Committee sat on either side of the chairman around the table. The shorthand writer and the other GMC support staff sat back from the table. Microphones were available for use by any speaker.

The proceedings moved along at their own legal pace, and there was a break for lunch. The proceedings then continued until the evening. Before going for his lunch, Andrew had a brief discussion with his leading counsel and solicitor in one of the side rooms that led to the Committee Suite on how they thought things were going. Mr. Powell-Jackson tried to be reassuring but was non-committal.

"This is just like television courtroom drama," Andrew said to himself, *"if not more arcane. It is going to be more of a tough call than I imagined.*

He nipped down to an Italian restaurant nearby, where he had a large pizza and a glass of white wine.

When the hearing resumed after the lunch break, Mr. Edward Powell-Jackson, on behalf of Mr. Andrew Wellington, mounted a spirited and ruthless rebuttal of all the charges against his client, whom he described as a "caring, respected surgeon of international repute." He laid into his Trust for scapegoating Mr. Wellington in its authoritarian drive to meet targets, get three stars, and become a Foundation Trust, regardless of how it impinged on real patient care "at the coalface."

The hearing carried on into the second day, Thursday, and ended by lunchtime. The members of the Committee then went into a closed session to consider their verdict. Their deliberations lasted just over four hours while Andrew and his legal team kicked their heels in their room annex close to the Committee Suite, drinking non-refreshing cups of coffee and tea, reading the day's *Times, Telegraph, Financial Times, Guardian*, etc., wondering which way the decisions would go.

At long last, an official knocked on their door, asking Mr. Andrew Wellington and his team to return to the Committee Suite, where the Committee members were already seated, for the formal delivery of the verdict of the Committee by the chairman, Professor Ian Farting-Bottom.

Andrew was asked to stand up as the chairman began his delivery:

Mr. Wellington, at your hearing just concluded, you were represented by Mr. Powell-Jackson of Leading Counsel, instructed by Hannington-Cliffe solicitors. Mr. Mathew Davies of Cresser-Brown, solicitors to the Council, appeared for the GMC.

The Committee has considered all the information before it is including the submissions by Mr. Powell-Jackson on your behalf, all the witnesses, and your own oral evidence.

*The Committee has come to the conclusion that on balance your actions did **not** cross the threshold of serious professional misconduct.*

The Committee wishes me to add that in the future, however, you must be more prudent about your financial relationship with multinational medical instruments companies. "The GMC office will advise you on any issues that may arise from this determination."

Andrew was mightily relieved by the Committee's determination and thanked his legal team profusely. He rang Alison straight away and she almost broke down in tears of relief and delight. The implications of an adverse determination she could hardly bring herself to dwell on.

Alison's twin sister, Sarah, was now not on speaking terms with her. And after the GMC verdict, Sarah said to herself with strong emotion, "I'm not finished with him yet!"

She began to hatch an elaborate plan to be alone with Andrew and drop her bombshell. A powerful current of emotion flowed through her, profound and unidentified. She did not know whether she was still attracted to him or repelled from him, but only that she was very deeply unsettled. It made her feel very alone.

A bit of retail therapy for starters, Sarah argued with herself.

A thin, warm rain was falling, and as the day grew dark, the rain came down harder. She paced up and down her hotel room in central London.

"Andrew, how could you?" she sobbed.

She sank back on her bed, then got up and went to the mirror, where she began brushing her hair, sniffling a little. She looked at her rounding stomach, then resumed brushing her hair frantically until her arm ached. Then she changed arms and mechanically went on brushing....

The sight of her bloom in the mirror failed to reassure her but only awakened the ache she felt whenever she thought of Andrew. She had found out where Andrew was staying in Kensington for the GMC hearing. That evening she put on her make-up carefully, dabbed on her favourite and delicate, if not expensive, perfume she bought in Paris, and slipped into alluring evening wear. She took a cab to Andrew's place. She pressed the flat's doorbell. Initially there was no response. At the third attempt, she was invited up. She had successfully disguised her voice and identity.

But as soon as Sarah entered Andrew's sitting room, they recognized each other.

"Good Lord, Sarah, what on earth are you doing here?"

"Just to congratulate you on the outcome of the GMC hearing."

"Really? No hard feelings?"

The old magic and frisson between them seemed to have returned as Sarah had hoped.

"You look gorgeous as ever!" Andrew said.

"Thank you."

There was a tense silence. Then Sarah put up her face quietly to be kissed. He looked at her for a moment as if he didn't understand. Then holding her in the hollow of his arm, he rubbed his cheek against her cheek's softness and then looked down at her for another long moment.

She smiled up at him, her hands playing conventionally with the lapels of his coat. Suddenly she drew closer to him. "I've something to tell you."

Andrew started. He was remembering too vividly their torrid liaison not many moons ago.

"I'm expecting your child. It's a boy. Here, you can have a look at the up-to-the-minute 3-D ultrasound scan. Keep it if you like. Some resemblance, isn't there?"

Andrew's face went pale, and then he just managed to grab a seat where Sarah was standing and fought to regain his composure. "How did it happen?"

"How do these things happen, Andrew? And you a doctor?"

"I thought-"

"Goodbye, Andrew," Sarah said as she took a resolute step toward the door.

He looked up at her as she took another elegant step in slow motion toward the door. She turned and looked at him again. He looked at her without the slightest idea as to what was in her head.

16

Andrew and Alison tried fervently to have a child in the first year of their marriage, but this was not to be. The events surrounding his last encounter with Sarah haunted Andrew relentlessly, but he never let on to Alison, who occasionally wondered why Andrew now and again withdrew himself into deep thought. His never-ending worry was not knowing what Sarah would do with the power she seemed to wield over him following the disclosure of the aftermath of their consuming liaison before he met Alison.

Sarah was now quite friendly with a London merchant banker, five years younger than herself. They met at a dinner party in the city. Being secretly in love felt glorious, and she didn't want the spell broken by telling the object of her affection.

Better to stick with the delicious expectation after my soul-destroying experience with Andrew, she said to herself.

And as if being in love was not the most marvelous fun in itself, not telling was utterly wonderful. It combined a kind of breathless excitement with anticipation to form a hyped-up state of pleasure-wired sensitivity. Anything could happen. Well, not as it happened with Andrew first time 'round.

It was like being on a constant edge of caffeine overload with none of the side effects. But it took a huge effort of will, and Sarah was sure she had the restraint and strength to keep it going. Things are never the same once they're out,

and she would have passed some fevered pitch of misty anticipation and stepped into the sunny uplands of frank and full
disclosure.

Sarah believed her undeclared love to be altogether
more contained and explosive. The confession was eternally
on the brink of her lips, or wherever these fabulous feelings
lived, only to be swallowed for another day, another opportunity. And once you have stifled the impulse to confess, the
practice of containment turns into a real challenge, and you
get rather adept at it.

Telling, Sarah asserted, meant facing up to some scary
realities. There is some good, safe fun to be had in the sealed
world of discreet silence. Yes, when she told Andrew, as in
a film, "I love you," things tumbled into place, and see how
"the End" scrolled up? Yes, the happily-ever-afters are more
complex. Alongside love comes loyalty-a tougher beast. And
tolerance, selflessness, forbearance-all challenging, all the realistic progeny of more whimsical love.

When you're very young in your twenties or earlier society's wheels are oiled for the smooth transition from
friendship to fiancé, all you mostly think about is founding a
family, putting down roots, and participating in evolutionary
dynamics. Here Sarah was now. Any new liaison could be a
bumpy, bumpy ride. No wonder her declarations for her new
love, Larry Russell, were hesitant.

Nonetheless, Sarah thought, *it is something volcanic,
exciting, and passionate. I'll have to run up a few flags about
how I feel. Ultimately not telling won't be me. That would be
risk averse. I am afraid of the consequences or the knock-
back, or the future, or all three. No coward's soul is mine. I
always go for the high stakes, don't I?*

17

Andrew and Alison were now living at an old grade-two list-ed farmhouse in Hampshire, which they bought some months after their marriage in Barbados. After the determination of the GMC's Committee on Professional Performance, Andrew wrote to his Trust and resigned his consultant post with the Trust. He was going to channel all his energies into his private practice at a nearby Nuffield private hospital.

The more than three-hundred-year-old flint-and-stone farmhouse had very thick walls and enjoyed a high degree of privacy in formal grounds and woodland of three acres. It also had an old bakery fireplace at the far end of the dining room, an Aga in the kitchen, and a laundry room. There was a spring-fed artisan well on the grounds with a stone-and-wood superstructure over it. Additionally, the property had a summer house, three-bay garage, paddocks, and stone gazebos.

Andrew was now working on a joint replacement implant for worn-out big-toe joints. It was a non-cemented hydroxy-apatite zirconium ceramic implant. And should the implant fail, the joint could easily be made comfortable and pain-free by fusing it with an intercalated bone graft. Early trials seemed promising, but attention to surgical details was crucial for good, functional results.

Andrew was invited as a guest speaker to a joint European Foot and Ankle Surgeons Society (EFAS) meeting with the British Orthopaedic Foot Surgeons Society (BOFSS) in Bristol to talk about his implant. He drove there in his brand-new Saab two-liter Vector auto sports saloon.

He was taken aback on arrival and check-in when he saw Sarah there as a senior sales representative of a much bigger orthopedic instruments company than she had previously worked for when they first met. She caught up with him during a coffee break, took him aside to a side room, and informed him about the birth of their son in a private clinic in London a couple of months back.

"Hello, Sarah," Andrew began uncertainly.

"Hello, Andrew," Sarah replied.

"You 're looking well."

"Thank you, Andrew. My baby son has been named William. Your name does not appear on his birth certificate."

"Ehmm…."

"Don't worry. Alison does not know you are the father."

"And who did you put down as the father?"

"That's not really your concern, is it?

"I presume there's a new man in your life, then."

"You presume right. His name is Larry Russell."

Andrew suddenly felt a sharp twinge of intense jealousy but tried very hard not to show it. "Nice chap?"

"Very much so. He is a merchant banker in the city."

"I must get back to the meeting," Andrew said stiffly.

Later that afternoon, Andrew chaired a discussion called "How Long Do Total Ankle Replacements Last? When They Fail Why Do They Fail?"

In Andrew's opinion, based on the most recent reports, a ten-year survivorship of more than 80 percent was realistic. The outcome of ankle replacement could further improve in the future because of improved implants, more reliable instrumentation, and increased experience, but it could never reach a success rate over time comparable to that of hip or knee replacement. There were several reasons for this. The ankle, he maintained, was a part of a functional unit, and any ankle pathology involved other joints as well, particularly the subtalar joint.

Mal-alignment and instability of the talus within the mortice was extremely difficult to be sufficiently addressed. Once again, the neighboring joints could be involved in the pathologic process. Probably the biggest source of failures was the use of non-anatomic implants that did not use the whole resection surface for bony support, which could lead to subsidence of component.

Andrew's take on the subject's discussion was very well received by the audience, which included Sarah, who had slipped into the back of the auditorium as the discussion progressed. She late invited Andrew to her hotel accommodation in the Clifton area of Bristol for dinner that evening. He was two minds on whether or not to accept.

Any encounter with Sarah was always going to be a charged affair even if it started on terms of frigid courtesy. The chemistry between them was unpredictable. There was a nervous constriction in his throat every time he thought about her since their break-up.

He duly arrived at the hotel Sarah was booked into by her company carrying a bouquet of quite expensive flowers. He felt a sense of excitement. He breathed deeply, with a sense of inhaling rarefied air.

"How is William?" Andrew quickly inquired at the doorstep.

"He's doing fine, thanks," Sarah replied.

"Sarah," Andrew began gently, "I don't... I simply don't know what to say...."

"Don't just stand there, Andrew. Do come in."

There was a pause as they moved inside her well-appointed hotel suite. Andrew could sense Sarah's initial confidence leave her. It was as if earlier, she had bolstered her self-assurance with a reserve of will, but now the reserve was gone and boldness with it. Sarah sat herself down in a settee and in a small, uncertain, voice she said, "You think I've not missed you all this time?"

She held out her hands toward him. He took them and stood facing her, and suddenly their fingers interlaced. She put up her face to be kissed, and he leaned toward her, He intended just to brush her cheek, but she put up her lips to his and, as they touched her arms wound tightly around him.

Dimly in his mind, an alarm bell jangled. Her body pressed against him; the sense of contact was electric. Her slim fragrance was immediate and breathtaking. Her perfume filled his nostrils. It was impossible, at that moment, to sustain his wish not to betray Alison. He felt his body awaken excitedly, his senses swim. The alarm bell was almost silenced.

Resolutely, however, he forced himself away. Taking Sarah's hand gently, he told her, "I must go." He went down the hotel steps, scarcely knowing they were there.

18

Andrew decided to drive back to Hampshire that evening, his mind in turmoil. While driving on the M3 motorway in the final stage of his journey, he darted alarmed glances at the driver of a white Vauxhall transit van that had made repeated attempts to overtake him. The driver was seen hunched over the wheel of his van and was manifestly pumping the accelerator to try and coax maximum gasp of power from his unsteady vehicle.

Something was evidently amiss beneath the bonnet of the vehicle or with the driver. He overtook Andrew's car dangerously, and then the van's engine spluttered and gave up the ghost. Andrew tried to take evasive action but to no avail. A multiple pile-up ensued. The driver of the Vauxhall van was killed instantly. It emerged he had been on illegal drugs and his breath reeked of booze.

Andrew was seriously injured and was rushed by ambulance to Winchester Hospital. He had suffered a moderate head injury with loss of consciousness, and the ambulance paramedic crew had reported his Glasgow Coma Scale score as 14/15. His car had rolled over and was badly dented. There was a suggestive rib fracture on the left side of his chest with local pain on attempted deep breathing, and his lower back and left ankle hurt.

He was admitted to the Intensive Care Unit. His X-rays, CT, and MRI scans confirmed a couple of left-side rib fractures, no pneumothorax, no skull fracture, no significant brain injury, minor stable compression wedge fracture of his first lumbar vertebra with no neurology, and a sprained left ankle.

The hospital got in touch with Alison soon after Andrew's admission, and she drove down to the hospital straight away. By then Andrew had regained consciousness but was under continued observation and monitoring, plus intravenous drip lines. Alison was allowed to be by his bedside, and he took a little while to be aware of her presence. He then forced a smile and nodded.

"It will be all right, darling. I am here." Alison spoke very softly to Andrew, who then smiled more broadly.

Andrew's recovery from his injuries was remarkably rapid to everyone's surprise, especially the medical and nursing staff. He seemed very determined to get going right from the start. He was discharged home with an initial lumbar surgical corset support alongside a programmed remedial physiotherapy course, which he quickly decided to carry on himself with astonishing results.

19

Alison arranged for a holiday break in Italy to help complete Andrew's recovery. They flew to Florence and booked into a four-star hotel on a quiet piazza just by the Ponte Vecchio.

"Have you been in Florence before, Alison? You seem to know so much about it."

"I have, actually, darling."

"Tell me more."

"Well, the Ponte Vecchio you can just about see from this window is open to pedestrians only. It is lined with quaint medieval-looking houses, and its fame saved it from damage in 1944 during the Second World War, although numerous ancient buildings at either end were blown up instead, in order to render it impassable. Near the site of the Roman crossing, which was a little further upstream, it was the only bridge over the Arno until 1218."

"Fascinating!"

"The present bridge of three arches was reconstructed after a flood in 1345. The bridge on this site has been lined by shops since the thirteenth century. An edict issued by the Grand Duke Ferdinand I in 1593 established that the butchers' shops and grocery shops here should be replaced by those of goldsmiths and silversmiths."

"The present jewelers' shops," Alison continued, "have pretty fronts with wooden shutters and awnings and overhang the river supported on brackets. The excellent jewelers here maintain the skilled tradition of Florentine goldsmiths, whose work first became famous in the fifteenth century."

"Amazing, Alison."

"Many of the greatest Renaissance artists trained as goldsmiths," she continued, "and included Ghiberti, Brunelleschi, and Donatello. The most famous Florentine goldsmith, Benvenuto Cellini, is aptly recorded with a bust in 1900 in the middle of the bridge."

"Above the shops on our left," Alison demonstrated, "can be seen the round windows of the Corridoio Vesariano. On the corner of a house is a sundial and worn inscription of 1345. The Corridoio Vesariano leaves the bridge supported on elegant brackets in order not to disturb the Torredei Mannelli, the medieval angle tower, which defended the bridge and was restored after the War."

As they held hands looking out of their hotel window, Andrew's tummy rumbled noisily.

"Darling, you hardly touched your breakfast this morning. No wonder your tummy is thundering!"

"Too true. I am feeling peckish now, though."

"Not to worry. I know a place down the street where you can still sample traditional Florentine cuisine with abundant use of Tuscan olive oil, the best in Italy, and elaborate meat dishes that are cooked slowly in a tomato sauce."

"Yummy!"

"If you are up to it, you can work your way through the hors d'oeuvres (*antipasti*), the first courses (*primipiatti*), the main courses (*second piatti*), fish (*pesce*) which can be expensive here, and the desert (*dolce*). Italians usually prefer fresh fruit for dessert, and sweets are considered the least important part of the meal. There is cheese (*formaggi*) and wine. The world-famous Chianti red wine is made from a careful blend of white and black grapes grown in a limited area of the Chianti region between Florence and Sienna."

The family-owned restaurant surpassed Andrew's culinary expectations. They started off with *crostini*-small pieces of toast with a type of pâté made out of chicken livers, capers, and anchovies. This was followed by minestrone thick vegetable soup.

For the main course, Andrew went for *Bistecca alla Fiorentina,* a large T-bone steak grilled in one piece-while Alison chose a fish item: *orata alla grigla*- grilled bream fish. For dessert they had *Macedonia*-fresh fruit salad, then assorted cheese including *gorgonzola*- a delicious, strong, creamy cheese made from whole cow's milk-and *Parmigiano-Reggiano,* a best-quality Parmesan cheese made in the districts of Parma and Reggio Emilia. Finally, they shared a bottle of Chianti red wine-*Chianti classico gallo nero.*

20

The next morning, they met a couple from the U.S.A. at breakfast, Alan and Isabelle Spitzer. Isabelle, a socialite from New York, immediately took a shine to Andrew. Alan was a senior partner in an accountancy firm in New York. They had just arrived in Florence from Venice, where they had stayed in a five-star hotel that was apparently one of the oldest fifteenth century palaces on the main waterway with a terrace directly on the Grand Canal. It was also a few minutes' walk from St. Mark's Square.

"Hi, Andy!" Isabelle said enthusiastically after their introductions across the breakfast table. "I like your tie and your shirt."

"Thank you."

"Where did you by them?" Isabelle pressed on.

"I can't quite remember. I think Alison got them for me in Regent Street, London."

"Good taste! The tie looks like pure silk. Can I feel it?"

"Of course."

"Your face looks familiar, Alison," Alan joined in, "Have I seen you somewhere before?"

"I'm not so sure," Alison replied evasively.

But Alison took little time to recollect her encounter with Alan some years back when she was a Wall Street fund manager handling the funds of Alan's accountancy firm. Alan had tried to proposition her then with romantic flannel and monetary bribes.

"You are just a professional collector of these romantic moments, aren't you?" Alison had suggested to Alan at that time.

"What's wrong with that?"

"I'm not going to be one of them."

"I'm at the Astoria Hotel if you change your mind."

"I won't."

Alison mused how weird it all was, crossing paths again like this in Florence, of all places. Mr. Spitzer, she recollected, had a good head for figures but was rather full of himself and boring. He was of medium height, middle-aged, and balding noticeably. His girth had begun to spread significantly.

Isabelle was quite different. She lived in today, this minute, and if the past or the future caught at her, struggled helplessly in moods that, while watching her you could give a name to, but she herself did not relate to the circumstances of her life. She had a strong fear of herself, as many active people do.

But whatever the human climate to which she had been exposed in her life had done to her psyche, her body was entirely itself, sure and beautiful. She was a loving woman in bed, clever and full of tender enthusiasm. "Now just wait," she would say, "just wait a minute…" as if her caresses were carefully prepared surprises that should not be discovered before the right moment.

Her whole body would burn with a steady warmth of energy, even while she slept, and only her buttocks and her breasts were cool, the way some people's hands are always cool.

She had set her sights on Andrew and was determined to get him.

She had arranged for the hotel to prepare sumptuously packed picnic lunches and invited Andrew and Alison to join her and Alan on a pleasant stroll through the compact city to include the superb Uffizi Gallery, the historic Accademia that exhibits the well-known statute of David, Florence's impressive cathedral, which boasts one of the most photographed structures in Florence: the Brunelleschi's dome or cupola. They would also stroll past the Piazza della Signoria with its exquisite statues and then Piazzale Michelangelo.

Her plan was to finish the stroll in the gardens of Viale Machiavelli, where she planned to make her move on Andrew.

It was an ideal, fine, sunny day with a slight breeze, and they all got into the spirit of the walk and eventually arrived at the gardens off the Viale Machiavelli as she planned.

Isabelle's cunning machinations to be alone with Andrew appeared to be succeeding as she took his arm seemingly to show him the exotic flowers in the gardens. She then deliberately tripped near a bush and shouted, "Damn it, I think I've done my right ankle."

"Let's have a look." Andrew quickly offered to help.

"Don't worry, Andy, I'm sure I'll be all right," she half-protested, watching his reaction very carefully.

"Nonsense. Let's just make sure."

As Andrew stooped down to have a look, Isabelle casually lifted up her skirt to expose her knickerless upper thigh and crotch. He was taken aback somewhat but soon regained his composure.

"I'm sure there are no broken bones. Just a minor ankle sprain, perhaps," Andrew declared.

"So sorry to be such a nuisance."

"No problem. Can you manage to put weight on it?"

"Just give me a hand, then."

As Andrew turned to do this, Isabelle leaned over awkwardly and fell on top of Andrew where she remained for a very long time, her cheek against his cheek, her lips hungrily seeking his.

Andrew scrambled free, and Isabelle recovered quickly enough to walk back, with hardly any limp, with Andrew to where Alan and Alison were having their picnic sandwiches in strained silence.

Yes, love is dangerous and intoxicating, Isabelle mused to herself. *But it gives one the most complete sense of being alive, more deliciously alive than you have ever been before, so that squelching it is simply out of the question.*

Isabelle first fell in love with a thump at the age of fifteen. He was a baseball player, much older than herself, and a friend of the family. She herself was more mature physically than her age would suggest and often pretended to be eighteen years of age.

This first love, Douglas, struck Isabelle as having a tremendous and infectious zest for life, which would make him such a good value as a husband, but she also thought it was likely to make him an unfaithful one, but this didn't even begin to sober her. She adroitly brushed aside the discordant thought that the intoxication of "being in love" was caused more often by the nature and needs of the person loving than by the merits of the beloved, so it would be amazingly good luck if they suited each other as well as believed they would.

When they got back to their hotel, Isabelle flirtatiously whispered to Andrew, "See you later, Andy. You have such tender healing hands. My ankle is almost mended now, thanks to you."

Andrew made no reply.

As soon as Alison rejoined him in their hotel apartment, however, she wasted no time in intimating it was time to leave Florence for home. She was not unaware of Isabelle's interest in Andrew, and Alan made her uncomfortable.

"Such a pleasant walk. Florence never ceases to amaze me, Andrew."

"Yes darling, and the weather is glorious."

"And the Spitzers seem such fun," she continued, eyeing Andrew suspiciously.

Andrew was silent.

"How about a brief stopover at Verona on our way back? I promised myself if opportunity arose, to see this romantic city since studying the works of Shakespeare in the Sixth Form at school. Apparently, the city was a favourite of Roman Emperors and liked to be known as the Dignified City, *La Denga*. Alison continued: "And of course, see Juliet's balcony and Tomb."

"Why not, Alison?"

"How about tomorrow? There is a daily flight from there to Gatwick once we get to the city."

Alison's plan was actually a relief to Andrew. It made it easier for him not to succumb to the determined attentions of Isabelle, which were quite flattering.

They decided on a train journey from Florence to Verona after checking out of their hotel just before midday without meeting the Spitzers again. They booked into a central four-star hotel very close to the Roman Arena and Via Mazzini, reputedly the best shopping street in Verona and a comfortable base for easy exploration of the city. From their hotel, there was an overview of the Adige River, which flowed swiftly through the city center. Luckily for them, the Verona Opera Festival had just started, the open-air opera season in Verona's magnificent Roman Arena (one of the most impressive after the Colosseum in Rome) with a production of *Aida* taking place within the arena's famous arched walls. The open-air opera season is now a major event on the international calendar. They managed to obtain two numbered seats.

Whether it was the sheer escape from the Spitzers or the romantic atmosphere of Verona, Alison felt particularly turned on during the couple of days they stayed in Verona. She went shopping around Piazza Bra and bought some rather slinky and provoking lingerie, as well as expensive, beguiling perfume.

Andrew was totally bowled over at bedtime. They did it several times- and for much longer while in Verona, with Alison as inventive and proactive as never before. Andrew's post-accident recovery therapy was complete!

21

They flew back to London Gatwick full of smiles and contentment.

"It was a lovely break, Andrew."

"Sure was. Many thanks."

"I feel a new woman."

"So do I. I mean, a new man. Thanks again." He fleetingly thought about Isabelle. He wondered what she would make of their disappearing act.

They unpacked slowly and felt like savouring an Italian take-away instead of doing any cooking and washing up, the dishwasher having packed up just before they departed for Italy. They enjoyed a delightful fare of lobster spaghetti washed down with one of the bottles of wine they had bought in Italy. They retired early to bed and quickly dozed off in tranquil and affectionate cuddle.

A few weeks later, Alison became aware that her breasts were firmer and more swollen. She visited the loo more often and also had morning sickness.

"I think I'm pregnant," she murmured excitedly to herself and wasted no time in going to the chemist's to buy a testing kit. It was strongly positive.

She kept the news to herself for a while. Andrew, however, was betimes puzzled by Alison's increasingly contrary behavior toward him, often provoking him into inexplicable arguments, and then she would slam the door in his face and cry, "You git! You don't really love me or care about a jot about me!"

One afternoon Andrew pulled open one of the cupboards in the bathroom, and a pregnancy testing kit dropped on the floor. He soon realised the probable reason Alison was behaving the way she was lately. He went and bought her a lovely bunch of flowers.

"Is this a guilt offering? What have you been up to, Andrew?"

"You are pregnant, aren't you?"

Alison looked down on the floor for a while, saying nothing. Then she suddenly began to smile impishly, leaped up, and hugged Andrew, with tears of joy in her eyes. "Yes darling! I'm so sorry for being so beastly to you for the past couple of weeks. I've had to pinch myself that I'm really pregnant after all those failed expectations and dashed hopes in the recent past. It is still early days, darling."

"Pessimist!"

"Realist!"

He embraced her passionately.

"Now be careful!" She teased him happily.

"Me? Never!"

She looked longingly into his eyes and, resting her head on his shoulder, began to cry. Andrew carried her gently to their bed, sat beside her, and hugged her with tenderness.

Some weeks later, Andrew and Alison went to a private clinic in Winchester to see a gynecologist friend of theirs, Mr. Bowden-Walker, who did an ultrasound scan on Alison. This suggested Alison was carrying twins.

"Good heavens, Alison, you never do things by halves!" Andrew quipped.

"Yes, but I did not tango by myself to make the twins, you smart Alec!" Alison gibed back.

"You win!"

"Of course, I always do. You don't even have to carry them. Better shut up!"

"Yes, my bossy lady!"

A couple of months later, when Alison saw Mr. Bowden-Walker again she came home with an astonishing 3-D ultrasound colour picture of the twins, whose facial features were readily discernable. She also knew the sex of the twins but for now decided to keep the secret to herself.

Alison developed a pica craving for things chalky, like some antacid tablets, and for pickled onions and broccoli. But these cravings only lasted a couple of months.

Meanwhile Andrew got back to work with gusto. He had secured sessions at an independent foot and ankle service hospital in London, where with hard work he was now earning more than he was at his earlier NHS Trust hospital position.

All seemed to be going very well with both Alison's pregnancy and his work. But one Monday afternoon, during a rather busy outpatient clinic, a call came through from Sarah Hopkins. She sounded desperate. Their son, William, had been admitted as an emergency to the Great Ormond Street Children's Hospital in London with suspected meningococcal meningitis.

"That's all I need now," Andrew said aloud to himself. The previous night he'd had a falling out with Alison over a trivial matter that got blown out of all proportion, and she would not speak to him until he apologised.

The last thing he wished was for his fathering of William to emerge in such an awkward fashion. Perhaps it was just Alison's topsy-turvy hormones playing up. He had to be understanding and patient. But there was no predicting what she would do right then if she found out about William.

"I'd like you to come down straight away," Sarah had demanded on Andrew's mobile phone's voice mail.

He wrapped up his clinic as quickly as he could and drove to the Great Ormond Street Hospital to find William in a very bad way. He had drip lines on and was responding slowly to treatment.

Sarah was very agitated. Her partner, Larry Russell, was away in U.S.A. on a business trip. William's illness came on so suddenly. Sarah initially thought it was a bad cold until she observed the telltale spots and rushed him to hospital.

Andrew was very troubled. There was no doubt William bore a striking resemblance to himself, and that made his attempts to feign indifference to his separation from the child even more heartbreaking.

"Do something! You are the big doctor," Sarah shouted at Andrew.

"I'm sure he's in good hands, Sarah." Andrew tried to calm things down.

"What if he dies?"

"He won't die. The doctors here are the best."

"I'll blame you if things go wrong for William. You should have been here earlier."

"I came as soon as I could."

"Not soon enough."

Sarah froze into a brooding silence. She had never gotten over her break up with Andrew and then his marriage to her twin sister. And things had not been rosy in the bedroom with Larry, her partner, and she secretly ceased to fancy him and resorted to tricks like going to bed very late, hoping he was asleep.

Larry had hoped to raise a family with Sarah. She agreed initially but subsequently changed her mind. Larry was very tactile, but Sarah did not reciprocate. As she began to withdraw from intimacy, this was always accompanied by excuses. Something was always wrong-and Larry poured a huge amount of time, effort, and money into "solving" all the "problems" Sarah invented.

Eventually she simply said it was not what she wanted. It seemed Larry had to accept her wishes in the matter of physical affection while she was never really prepared to recognize his. Larry had a brief affair and a couple of one-night stands, of which Sarah knew nothing. He was fully aware they had very different physical needs and would have accepted a compromise, but no such thing was on offer, nor was the subject open for discussion.

It began to dawn on Larry that the trouble was that all of us have a vague idea of what marriage and partnership is supposed to be like, and it is usually doomed to disappointment in varying proportions and scale.

Despite all the efforts of the treating doctors, William's early improvements were not sustained. He died on the third day of admission. Sarah was inconsolable. She retreated into herself after Andrew had driven her home and stayed the night at her place to comfort her.

Following William's death, Sarah's sleep became very disturbed, and she would wake up about three in the morning with her mind working overtime as if she had some unfinished business. She then found it difficult to get back to sleep.

When she managed to get some sleep, the quality was poor and she would wake in the morning unrefreshed. She had begun to lose her appetite for food, though paradoxically she would overeat on a few occasions. She tended to be constipated, and her weight on the bathroom scales went up and down. She suffered a curious mixture of lethargy, restlessness, and agitation.

Tears would flow over little things. Her mood would vary throughout the day, tending to be worse in the mornings. She felt awfully guilty about William and then would become very hostile and angry at Andrew, seemingly for no reason. Her concentration, self-esteem, and self-image plummeted. Unusually for her, she became indecisive and dithering with a lack of drive -disengaging and withdrawing from life.

22

When Sarah learned that her twin sister, Alison, was expecting twins soon, her bitterness toward Andrew intensified. During her sojourn in the U.S.A, she had legally acquired a snub-nose .44 caliber Smith and Wesson M624 double-action revolver, which she had learned to fire adroitly for personal defense. She was then one of the best shots in town. She still had the revolver hidden in one of her cupboard drawers.

Sarah arranged for Andrew to come over to her place for a special evening meal. A newly framed and enlarged photo of William was placed at the center of the dining room table.

She bought two vintage expensive bottles of finest French *Moet et Chandon* champagne and was dressed in gorgeous and revealing evening wear, dabbing on her favourite French Dior perfume, which Andrew used to adore. She was in a carefully suppressed agitated mood as she got ready her specialty dish of French Omelet filled with grated cheese; sliced mushrooms, cooked gently in butter for five minutes; chopped ham; cubes of fried potato; an onion, finely sliced and gently fried. For pudding, she had prepared a summer fruit tart.

Andrew walked into Sarah's flat in a somewhat anxious mood, and he pointedly did not tell Alison he was going to Sarah's.

"Come in, darling," Sarah greeted him excitedly.

"You look beautiful."

"Thank you."

"Something smells nice. Makes one feel peckish."

"Nothing, really," Sarah added modestly.

She looked at Andrew disconcertingly straight in the eye. She was suddenly seized by irrepressible and extreme anxiety as her persistent "replays" and flashbacks of William's last days struck again. She went all quiet and distant on Andrew.

She came to with an exaggerated show of bonhomie and invited Andrew to sit down opposite her on the dining room table. She passed one of the bottles of champagne to Andrew for him to open, and he did so expertly.

"Well done, Andrew. You were always good at this type of thing."

They tucked into Sarah's nosh with manifest relish, rekindling the spirit of old times as they knocked back the two bottles of champagne in record time, Sarah drinking far more of it than Andrew. She was now swinging from being euphoric to being down in the dumps and close to tears.

"Don't desert me tonight, Andrew." Sarah said in a dead-pan sort of voice.

Andrew began to get worried somewhat but could not put his finger on what exactly.

As the evening wore on, Sarah became more irritable and agitated. "Come to bed with me, Andrew." Her voice, though now rather imperious, was still seductive as of old.

Andrew followed. His conscience tortured him to no avail.

It was all rather woozy as they got into bed, but Sarah's carefully rehearsed plan was not going to be thwarted, She did all the right things to get Andrew remarkably horny and hard-on for lovemaking, which seemed perfect as Andrew very soon dropped off to a satisfied deep sleep.

Sarah's countenance suddenly and inexplicably froze into a mask-like frown. As if she was an automaton, she unemotionally retrieved the loaded Smith and Wesson revolver she had hidden in one of the drawers of a cupboard and returned to the bedroom.

She kissed Andrew on the forehead, whispering, "I will always love you, Andrew. To eternity," crossed herself, and shot him in the forehead with lethal precision. She then bestrode his torso, ripped open the front of her nightdress, threw her head back, and shot herself into the roof of her open mouth, slumping forwards onto the front of Andrew's chest.

23

It is now exactly a year since Sarah and Alison's parents, Marjorie and Philip Hopkins died in a terrible M25 motorway accident on their way to Heathrow airport for their British Airways holiday flight to Greece.

Despite their often sharp differences and disagreements Alison had planned a conciliatory chat with Sarah for that day but repeated attempts to reach her twin sister failed. Alison instinctively felt something out of the ordinary was going on as a fitting memorial for their parents had been discussed a couple of weepy times previously.

Alison now on edge was totally devastated when she received a text message from Dr. Michael Elliott-Smith, a very close friend of Andrew Wellington regarding his tragic and shocking death. Michael tried to spare her the details, but Alison instinctively guessed what must have happened. She knew her twin sister all too well.

Dr. Elliott- Smith and Andrew Wellington had both been Senior Registrars at the prestigious Royal National Orthopaedic Hospital (RNOH) at both the Stanmore, Brockley Hill London Borough of Harrow set up and the town set up at Great Portland Street. The RNOH is a major teaching center and around 20% of orthopedic surgeons in the UK receive training there.

Dr. Elliott-Smith specialized in knee surgery and had worked closely with Professor Trickey, a Senior Knee Surgery Consultant at RNOH. Interviews for National Health Service (NHS) Consultant posts were often grueling for qualified Senior Registrars after their training and Michael got through one of these on his third attempt.

This allowed him to acquire a very profitable private knee clinic at London's Harley Street, specializing in knee trauma and especially anterior cruciate ligament (ACL) injury reconstruction and he soon became the go-to place for professional footballers and rugby players with any suspicion of damage to the ligament.

He also had a satellite clinic on Merseyside in Liverpool.

24

Alison was still badly shaken by the details of Andrew's death. They had longingly wanted children of their own, but Alison had had two miscarriages. She always adored Andrew and felt sure Andrew felt the same about her. She was wretchedly convinced her twin sister Sarah did what she did to get one over her. But she was now determined to rise above her simmering fury over their secret affair.

Frantically she searched through Andrew's papers and could hardly believe what she discovered. Among other things Andrew had bafflingly deposited his sperm specimen at a London clinic following Alison's second miscarriage, stipulating that the sperms were for Alison alone and were to be destroyed after his stated period of time. Alison just could not figure it all out. However, she was now more determined to have Andrew's baby via IVF assisted conception.

The following week she booked an appointment to see her General Practitioner (GP), Dr. Kimberley Price who looked at her medical history and gave her a physical examination. She also recommended some lifestyle changes to help fertility prior to referral to a fertility specialist.

At her first appointment with the specialist, Dr. Clinton Darcy, he investigated the number of eggs in Alison's body (her ovarian reserve) to estimate how her ovaries will respond to IVF treatment. This was assessed by measuring substance called anti-mullerian hormone (AMH) in the blood sample she gave and by counting the number of egg-containing follicles known as antral follicle count (AFC) using the vaginal ultrasound scan she just had. A review appointment was made for three months to discuss treatment plans with Alison in detail including any support or guidance she may find helpful.

25

Dr. Elliott-Smith met his wife Amanda Parker at a New Year dance party in London. She had trained as a physiotherapist at St Thomas's hospital in London but was now the Superintendent Physiotherapist at another London Teaching Hospital. Her expertise in handling Michael's post-operative knee patients contributed to Michael's remarkable reputation for excellent results for anterior cruciate ligament (ACL) reconstruction.

Amanda's parents lived in a farmhouse near Winchester (Hampshire) and they had initially thought Amanda was very keen to be a doctor, having done so well in her A-Level exams in the necessary subjects.

A lecture during her training on the cardinal role of physiotherapy in disabled children sparked her interest in the care and management of children with cerebral palsy.

She recognized that the diagnosis, investigation, and management of cerebral palsy in childhood have a relevance not only for orthopedic surgeons and pediatricians but also for a wide range of treating agencies including physiotherapists like herself, affected individuals and their families, voluntary organizations concerned with neurologic disability, and in modern times, lawyers practicing in the medical negligence field.

Alison quickly became aware that all varieties of cerebral palsy have in common the fact that they present as evolving and changing disorders of movement and motor function, which occur secondarily to the affected individuals having some non-progressive abnormality of their immature brain.

Also, that the significant motor dysfunction of the various varieties of cerebral palsy evolves and changes dramatically with time. The youngest brain-damaged infants are with few exceptions overly floppy due to a central hypotonia associated with microcephaly, the persistence of primitive reflexes, and overly brisk tendon reflexes.

Overall, Amanda was convinced cerebral palsy was genetically determined with disorders arising during gestation and perinatally.

26

Amanda and Alison had become firm "bestie" friends as their husbands were. Alison said to herself that she needed a break to clear her head following Andrew's death. She quickly thought about Amanda joining her in her planned trip to Venice which she had visited before when she was single and loved it very much. Amanda was so delighted to be invited and said yes.

They took off from Stansted airport on a 13.10 Ryanair flight to Venice Marco Polo- Tessera arriving in late afternoon. They quickly checked into the five-star Hilton Molino Stucky Venice Hotel. After a good shower bath, they ordered room service drinks and began to plan things to do in Venice from museum-hop, island-hop, or simply hop into a restaurant and take it all in.

The next day they hit the Dorsoduro district which gave them a glimpse at the real Venice among fantastic attractions. They visited the Gallerie dell'Accademia and people-watched in the vibrant Campo Santa Margherita.

Next was the Teatro La Fenice, the city's most prestigious theatre first built in 1792. Fittingly it is adorned in dazzling red and gold.

They strolled around the dynamic neighborhood of Cannaregio the following day and explored the Jewish Ghetto, the Church of Madonna dell'Orio, and the Ponte delle Guglie. They later visited the Peggy Guggenheim Collection housed in Palazzo Venier dei Leoni on the Grand Canal and discovered works from around 200 artists including Pablo Picasso and Salvador Dali.

Continuing to tick off their bucket list of famous Venetian landmarks they hit the Canal Grande, a breathtaking hive of activity flanked by glorious Venetian architecture and landmarks along the Grand Canal including the Rialto Bridge.

Their cameras were ready when they arrived at the show-stopper, Piazza San Marco. Apparently, Napoleon called the famous square "the drawing room of Europe" with its splendid shops, cafes, and iconic buildings.

They could not miss the Gothic masterpiece of the Doge's Palace which overlooks both the Grand Canal and Piazza San Marco and was the historic seat of power for the Venetian Republic for more than 700 years.

Amanda and Alison took an elevator ride to the highest point in Venice atop the Campanile di San Marco - the bell tower a symbol of the Venetian landscape, offering incredible views across the lagoon.

27

Alison and Amanda's stay in Venice lasted ten days and when they got back to London Alison felt totally refreshed with a renewed zest for life. She cheerily went for her follow–up appointment with Dr. Clinton Darcy her fertility specialist who had some good news for her. Before she left for Venice, she had received medication to suppress her natural menstrual cycle followed by ten days of self-administered follicle-stimulating hormone (FSH) daily injections to increase the number of eggs her ovaries would produce. This means more eggs can be collected and fertilized. With more fertilized eggs the specialist has a greater choice of embryos to use in treatment. Also, Alison had vaginal ultrasound scans to monitor her ovaries.

About 36 hours before her eggs were due to be collected, she had a final hormone injection to help her eggs to mature. Shortly before she left for Venice, under some 20-minute sedation and ultrasound guidance, Alison's eggs were collected using a needle passed through the vagina and into each ovary.

The collected eggs were mixed in the laboratory with Andrew's donated sperm specimen. The good news that awaited Alison's return from Venice was that when her specialist checked some 20 hours later quite a few of the eggs had been fertilized!!

The fertilized eggs (embryos) continued to grow in the laboratory and Alison's new appointment was to decide when to transfer the best one or two chosen embryos via vaginal catheter into Alison's womb, a procedure that needs no sedation.

To help prepare the lining of the womb to receive the embryo hormone medicines a pessary placed inside the vagina was prescribed. Any suitable leftover embryo Alison and her specialist agreed to freeze for future IVF attempts.

However, all went well with the embryo transfer and Alison found herself with child weeks later following pregnancy blood and urine tests. Weeks later ultrasound scans confirmed a healthy boy fetus and the pregnancy progressed very well till uneventful vaginal delivery at term.

Alison had decided to name him Andrew Philip Hopkins, having now reverted to her maiden surname.

About the Author

Dr. William Agunwa was born in Enugu, the former capital of Biafra, Eastern Nigeria.

In his early years he won an open scholarship to the prestigious Government College Umuahia and the University of Glasgow Medical School. There he qualified with a Class Prize in surgery leading to house jobs with the Regius Professors of Surgery and Medicine.

He continued training at the Royal National Orthopaedic Hospital (at both the Stanmore and London locations) and became a Senior Fellow with the Royal College of Surgeons and the Royal Society of Medicine.

From there he continued working as a consultant for teaching hospitals in England, Scotland, and the Middle East, including King Khalid Military City Hospital in Jeddah, King Abdulaziz Airforce Military Hospital in Dhahran, and Riyadh Military Teaching Hospital in Saudi Arabia. He also worked as the Chief of Surgery at King Fahad Specialist Hospital in Medina.

Besides working in the Middle East, Dr. Agunwa has also widely traveled across Europe including the Balkans, the Nordic countries, the Irish Republic, Ulster and has made several trips to the USA.

As an author, Dr. Agunwa started writing even before his medical undergraduate days with minor publications in college and parish magazines. During his career, he continued to write articles for the British Medical Journal and the Journal of Accident Surgery, going on to publish his first novel, Jobs for the Boys, in 1990.

www.ingramcontent.com/pod-product-compliance
Lightning Source LLC
Chambersburg PA
CBHW071950190726
48293CB00004B/1413